For Amber,
one of the greatest givers I know.

Made with digital paint in Photoshop and lots of coffee.

Library of Congress Cataloging-in-Publication Data:
Names: Doerrfeld, Cori, author, illustrator.
Title: The giving day : a Cubby Hill tale / Cori Doerrfeld.
Description: New York : Abrams Books for Young Readers, [2020] | Audience: Ages 3 to 7. |
Summary: Cooper is excited to help his grandmother by delivering honey at the annual Great
Giving Festival, but one jar after another is ruined when he takes time to help his friends.
Identifiers: LCCN 2020018047 | ISBN 9781419744198 (hardcover) |
ISBN 9781683359043 (ebook)
Subjects: CYAC: Generosity—Fiction. | Helpfulness—Fiction. |
Festivals—Fiction. | Animals—Fiction.
Classification: LCC PZ7.D6934 Giv 2020 | DDC [E]—dc23
LC record available at https://lccn.loc.gov/2020018047

Printed and bound in U.S.A.
10 9 8 7 6 5 4 3 2 1

Abrams Books for Young Readers are available at special discounts when purchased
in quantity for premiums and promotions as well as fundraising or educational use.
Special editions can also be created to specification. For details,
contact specialsales@abramsbooks.com or the address below.

**ABRAMS** The Art of Books
195 Broadway, New York, NY 10007
abramsbooks.com

# The Giving Day

## A Cubby Hill Tale

### Cori Doerrfeld

Abrams Books for Young Readers

New York

Each year, everyone in Cubby Hill came together for the Great Giving Festival.

Some brought tasty treats like fresh donuts or ice cream.

Others brought art, games, or music to share. In tradition
with the giving spirit Cubby Hill was founded on, everyone brought
some way to give back and celebrate their community.

Cooper and his grandma always brought the final batch of honey
from their hives. This year, Cooper's grandma also thought he was old enough
to help her deliver it all over the festival. "*Bee* careful!" she said.
"Once this honey is gone, there's no more 'til spring!"

"Don't worry, Grammy Bea." Cooper was so excited.
"I'll make sure everyone gets their Great Giving gift! Because I'm . . ."

First up was the Bouncy family.

"Hey, Bobbi!" said Cooper. "I brought you some honey!"

"Thanks, Cooper!" Bobbi zipped by. "I'll get it in a second. We're trying to set up the bounce house, but my baby brothers keep getting in the way!"

Cooper had an idea.
"Don't worry! I'll watch them for you!
Super Cooper is the fastest bunnysitter in the universe!"

Cooper ran . . .

and jumped . . .

and did his best to keep the bunnies out of trouble.

But somehow,
they still got into Bobbi's jar of honey.

Suddenly, Cooper didn't feel very fast. "Sorry about the sticky situation.
I'll help clean them up and stop by later with another jar."

Next, Cooper saw his friend Henry unloading a cart
for his family's paint-a-pumpkin stand.
"Henry! I have some honey for you!"

"Oh . . . *hmph*." Henry grunted. "Thanks.
Just set it . . . *grph*, over there."

Cooper couldn't help but notice how heavy all the pumpkins looked.

"I'll help you carry those, Henry! Super Cooper is the strongest pumpkin picker in the universe!"

Together, Cooper and Henry moved pumpkins of all shapes and sizes.

Everything went great until the very last one.

The pumpkin landed right on Henry's honey.
Suddenly, Cooper didn't feel very strong. "Oh my gourd! I'm sorry!
I promise to bring you a new one!"

Cooper was determined to successfully deliver
the next jar of honey. So when he saw his friend
Stella, he rushed right over.

She looked frustrated.
"Is everything ok?" Cooper asked. "Will honey cheer you up?"

"Ack! I'm trying to figure out a glitch in our virtual-reality game.
I need someone to play it, but everyone in my family is afraid of heights!"

Cooper smiled. This was going to be fun. "I'll help you fix it!
Super Cooper is the bravest gamer in the universe!"

Cooper zoomed and buzzed while Stella typed
and tweaked until all the bugs were gone.

Or so they thought . . . "Now to get your honey!"

Suddenly, Cooper didn't feel very brave.

For the rest of the day, Cooper planned to be extra careful,
but he still almost bumped into Muffin and Muggy McMousie.

"Oh, Cooper!" Muffin was overjoyed. "Muggy and I went
to find a part for our ice-cream maker and got lost!"

Cooper didn't waste a second.

"Never fear! **SUPER COOPER** is here!"

Cooper got Muffin, Muggy, and the part for their ice-cream maker
back safe and sound. He almost felt like a real hero.

But then Cooper went to give them their honey . . .
"Oh no! It's all gone! I'll be right back."

Cooper ran as fast as he could to Grammy Bea's honey stand.

But he was too late! His friends were already there explaining everything to Grammy Bea. Not only had Cooper ruined every Great Giving gift so far, now his grandma would never trust him to deliver the rest of the honey. Suddenly, Cooper just felt defeated.

But then . . .

# SUPER COOPER RULES!

"They all came to thank you!" Grammy Bea smiled.

Cooper could hardly believe it. "For what?

Bobbi jumped up and down.
"You helped me with my baby brothers. Our bounce house is up because of you!"

Henry cheered. "Your help is the reason all of our pumpkins are ready to decorate!"

Stella twirled. "You helped make sure my game was bug-free!"

"And Muggy and I can never thank you enough," Muffin added,
"for helping us find our way home!"

Cooper watched as every single one of his friends
went off to help *him* deliver the rest of the honey.

"And I want to thank you too," Grammy Bea said.
"For always helping anyone and everyone who needs it."

"That's what makes you my Super Cooper—
the greatest gift giver in the universe."